THE

STAY-AT-HOME

BEARS

A Prowly *and* Growly Adventure

BY

Carol *and* Joyce Burbank

Carol Burbank (signature)

Zoe + Leif:
Enjoy!
love,
Prowly,
Growly
and
Flo.

Design BY Firebrand Creative

firebrandcreative.me

Storyweaving Press
P.O. Box 739
Accokeek, MD 20607

Contact: cburbank@storyweaving.com

ISBN 978-0-9966566-5-8
© 2020 Storyweaving Press

"Any day spent with you
is my favorite day.
So, today is my new
favorite day."

– WINNIE THE POOH

Dedicated to every friend of adventuring bears –
whether new fuzzies or ancient bare-naked teddies ...

May this book inspire you to new adventures together!

All of a sudden, we have new rules in our family.

Our first rule is "Wash Your Hands!"

I really want things
to get back to the way
they were.

I play with the bubbles
and cheer myself up.

Online school is weird.

"I miss recess and Hot Dog Tuesday," whispers Flo.

"I miss passing notes to Barry Bear," mutters Prowly.

"Flo, it's your turn to read," growls Mr. Bruin.

Online school is weird.

Mom asks Growly to wash the windows because they were all smudged from bear noses.

It's an important job!

While he polishes,
Growly waves at the dogs
walking their neighbors.

Dad asks Flo to clean up the porch.

"I am!" she says.

But she isn't.

Prowly hides in a corner and plays his favorite game.

There's plenty of time to sweep the kitchen later!

Flo thinks the dinosaur family should wash their hands, too.

She teaches them how so they will do it right.

We don't have to wear masks on the computer.

Brownie tells a joke. Growly laughs so hard he gets the hiccups.

Flo tells another joke. Everyone groans and giggles.

Then Cousin Bess arrives for a surprise visit.

"Can I come in?"

"Wait a minute. We have to get our masks."

We make so much noise that Mom sends us outside to play, six paws apart.

Everyone yells, "Roll the ball to me!"

The ball is so big, it almost knocks Growly over.

"Can we play hide and seek instead?" asks Growly.

Hide and seek is Growly's favorite.

He thinks he finds the best place to hide
in the garden.

But Cousin Bess sees
his mask.

"Tag!"

Flo hides in the geranium bush, and wins the game.

Then Mom tells us it's time to get ready for dinner.

Cousin Bess is going to eat with us.

The dinosaurs are having a handwashing party before dinner!

Cousin Bess has to rescue a T-Rex from the bubbles.

It's pizza night! Growly chooses the toppings because he was the only bear who did his chores.

"Sausage, peppers and pineapple – my favorite!"

"Eew," says Flo, and picks all the peppers off her piece.

It's been a perfect stay-at-home day.

ABOUT THE AUTHORS

Carol and Joyce Burbank are a mother–daughter team, creating both the story and the photography documenting Prowly & Growly's Adventures.

Carol Burbank is an educational consultant, writing coach, poet, playwright and journalist, as well as a children's book author.

She loves the playfulness and magic of creating stories around these beloved bears.

Joyce Burbank is a retired gifted education teacher, who specialized in supporting creativity and personal and intellectual exploration with elementary school students. The bears you'll meet in this book have been with Joyce since her childhood.

The Prowly & Growly Adventure Series has also been a wonderful adventure for both Carol and Joyce. This is their third collaboration, which started with Prowly Plans a Party, followed by Down East Summer: A Prowly and Growly Adventure, also published by Storyweaving Press. They hope this newest book helps inspire readers during these stay-at-home times.

ABOUT THE BEARS

Prowly and Growly are best friends, two ancient and much-loved bears with very little hair – but very big imaginations. This book also introduces their sister, Flo.

Prowly has always prowled at night, and any other time he can. He loves books and, since Growly can't read as well, Prowly usually reads aloud to his best friend. Growly, though shy, is nonetheless a brave explorer, as is Flo. Her alter ego is Super Chicken, a flying crime fighter. The trio loves to dress up in all sorts of costumes when they play together.

Together, they're always looking for their next Adventure. With a little help they always find one, and are happy to tell the tale.

CPSIA information can be obtained at www.ICGtesting.com
Printed in the USA
LVIW010217161020
668976LV00005B/33